W9-DFQ-845

VESTAVIA HILLS
PUBLIC LIBRARY

1112 Montgomery Highway
Vestavia Hills, Alabama 35216

Spring Sail

Written by Larry Dane Brimner • Illustrated by R. W. Alley

E
Brim L

The Child's World

Published in the United States of America by The Child's World®
PO Box 326 • Chanhassen, MN 55317-0326
800-599-READ • www.childsworld.com

Reading Adviser

Cecilia Minden-Cupp, PhD, Director of Language and Literacy, Harvard University Graduate School of Education, Cambridge, Massachusetts

Acknowledgments

The Child's World®: Mary Berendes, Publishing Director

Editorial Directions, Inc.: E. Russell Primm, Editorial Director and Project Manager; Katie Marsico, Associate Editor; Judith Shiffer, Assistant Editor; Matt Messbarger, Editorial Assistant

The Design Lab: Kathleen Petelinsek, Design and art production

Copyright © 2006 by The Child's World®
All rights reserved. No part of this book may be reproduced or utilized in any form or by any means without written permission from the publisher.

Library of Congress Cataloging-in-Publication Data

Brimner, Larry Dane.
  Spring sail / written by Larry Dane Brimner ; illustrated by R. W. Alley.
    p. cm. — (Magic door to learning)
  Summary: A child describes some of the sights and sounds of early spring.
  ISBN 1-59296-519-9 (lib. bdg. : alk. paper) [1. Spring—Fiction.] I. Alley, R. W. (Robert W.), ill. II. Title.
  PZ7.B767Spr 2005
  [E]—dc22   2005005363

A book is a door, a magic door.
It can take you places
you have never been before.
Ready? Set?
Turn the page.
Open the door.
Now it is time to explore.

Spring is the gentle *splish-splash*
of rain against my window.

4

Spring is rubber boots
and yellow slickers.

6

My big sister and
I chase gray clouds
from puddle to pool.
Splash!
Bits of gray clouds
fly out all around.

We sail newspaper boats
down the street

that becomes a river
that turns into the sea.

Then gray clouds
change to blue,
blue sky.

We scoop up
our soggy boats.

We try to find the
rainbow's end.

16

But all we see are the
first, small, green buds
on the branches of trees

20

and the bright,
red blossoms of tulips.

21

Spring remembers
the chill of winter,
but it is the promise
that summer will
soon be here.

Our story is over, but there is still much to explore beyond the magic door!

Want to sail your own newspaper boat? Grab a sheet of newspaper and have an adult help you to fold it into a boat. No need to wait for a spring shower—you can test your boat in your very own bathtub!

These books will help you explore at the library and at home:
Carr, Jan, and Dorothy Donohue (illustrator). *Splish, Splash, Spring.* New York: Holiday House, 2001.
Plourde, Lynn, and Greg Couch (illustrator). *Spring's Sprung.* New York: Simon & Schuster Books for Young Readers, 2002.

About the Author

Larry Dane Brimner is an award-winning author of more than 120 books for children. When he isn't at his computer writing, he can be found biking in Colorado or hiking in Arizona. You can visit him online at *www.brimner.com.*

About the Illustrator

R. W. Alley has illustrated more than seventy-five books for children and has authored five of these. Since 1997, he has served as the illustrator on Michael Bond's Paddington Bear series. Alley lives in Barrington, Rhode Island, with his wife and two children. He often visits local elementary schools to discuss how words and pictures come together to form books.

VESTAVIA HILLS
LIBRARY IN THE FOREST
1221 MONTGOMERY HWY
VESTAVIA HILLS, AL 35216
205-978-0155